Who Lives Here?

BOOK TWO: Forests

Words by Dawn Baumann Brunke
Art by Mary A. Shafer

NorthWord
PRESS, INC

Box 1360, Minocqua, WI 54548

AUTHOR'S DEDICATION

This book is for my niece, the star lady, Anais.

Special thanks to David Personius for his creativity, persistence,
and enthusiasm in providing the idea upon which the *Who Lives Here?* series was based.

© 1993 NorthWord Press, Inc.
Box 1360, Minocqua, WI 54548

Edited by Greg Linder
Designed by Russell S. Kuepper

Cover photo by Robert W. Baldwin
Inside photos: pp. 9, 18, 21, 33, and 34, Robert W. Baldwin; p. 6, Michael H. Francis; p. 10, David M.
Dennis, Tom Stack & Associates; p. 13, Diana Stratton, Tom Stack & Associates; p. 22, Thomas
Kitchin, Tom Stack & Associates; p. 25, Robert C. Simpson, Tom Stack & Associates; p. 30, Joe
McDonald, Tom Stack & Associates; p. 37, Tom Stack, Tom Stack & Associates.

For a free catalog describing NorthWord's
line of nature books and gifts, call 1-800-336-5666

ISBN 1-55971-153-1

Printed in Hong Kong

WHAT'S A HABITAT?

The place where an animal lives is called its **habitat**.

People live in different kinds of places. You might live in a small log cabin by a lake, or in a tall apartment building on a busy street. You might live in a two-story house next to other houses on a block, or in a cottage at the edge of a field. Some people live in trailers, and some people live in farmhouses. Some people live in igloos built of packed snow, and some people live in castles. We all need to live somewhere.

Animals need places to live, too. An animal habitat is an area, like a neighborhood, where certain kinds of animals live. A habitat could be a forest, a lake, or a meadow. It could be a field, a pond, or a marsh. Every animal has a habitat where it's most comfortable, and where it has the best chance of surviving. More than anything else, a habitat is a home.

In this book, you'll color 12 animals that live in forest habitats. The three habitats are needleleaf forests, broadleaf forests, and mixed forests.

If you'd like to know more, just turn the page!

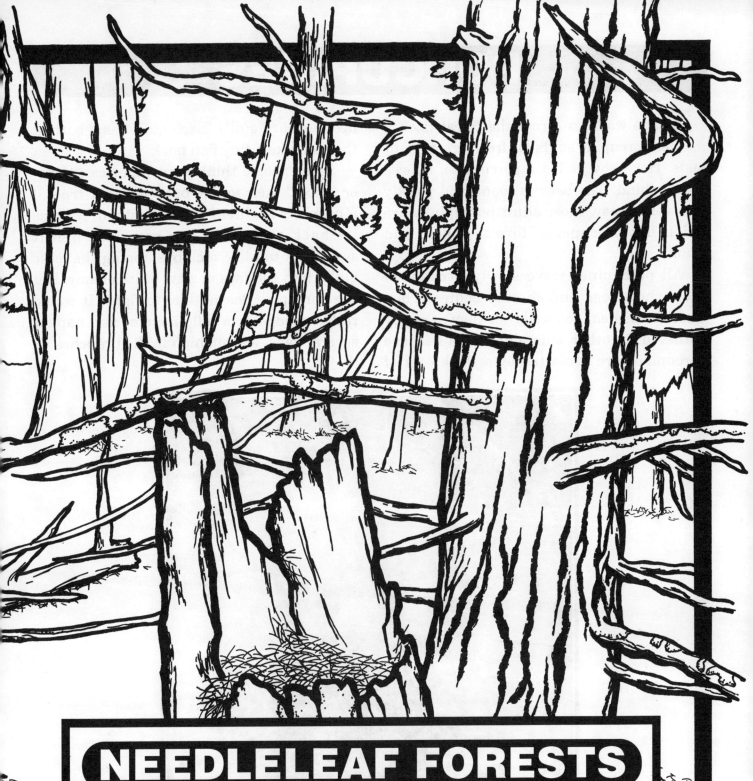

NEEDLELEAF FORESTS

Long before grasses, wildflowers, shrubs, or other trees grew on the earth, there were needleleaf forests. Needleleafs are trees with thin, pointy leaves. We call their leaves needles. The pine trees that many people decorate at Christmas are needleleafs. Needleleaf trees are sometimes called *conifers*, because many have cones dangling from their branches. Instead of dropping all of their leaves in autumn, needleleafs lose only a few needles at a time. Because new needles grow in their place, most needleleaf trees stay green all year. So they're also called *evergreens*.

PORCUPINES

As she waddles across the forest floor, a mother porcupine sniffs for fresh green plant buds. Her baby, called a porcupette, follows close behind. The baby is round and prickly and very noisy. Most adult porcupines are quiet, but porcupettes love to squeal and grunt.

All porcupines move slowly, because of their short legs and chunky bodies. They can't see or hear too well, but they're rarely bothered by other animals. That's because porcupines are protected by a thick coat of needle-sharp quills. Each quill has a barb at the end, like a tiny fish hook.

Some people think porcupines can throw or "shoot" their quills, but that's not true. If a porkie is frightened by an animal, it turns its back and grunts or growls. Then it swings its tail like a club, slapping the loose quills into the face or paw of its enemy. But the porcupine doesn't like to fight. It would rather trudge up a tall pine tree and nap for several days, way up high in the branches.

LYNX

After dark, a lynx climbs along fallen trees and mossy rocks in the forest, hiding behind bushes near a trail used by small forest animals. Because lynx can't run too fast, they like to jump out and surprise their prey. If a snowshoe hare hops along the trail, the lynx pounces on it and captures the startled hare.

Lynx are shy creatures. They like to prowl and live alone. They sleep in hollow logs during the day and hunt at night. They'll eat squirrels and grouse, but their main food is snowshoe hares. The number of lynx in a forest depends on the number of snowshoe hares. When the forest contains many snowshoes, more lynx are born to hunt the hares. When there are fewer hares, fewer lynx are born.

Lynx stay warm all winter because of their thick, golden-gray fur. Their big, bushy paws are like snowshoes, letting lynx walk right across mounds of deep snow without sinking. All lynx have tufts of hair on the tops of their ears, and short, black-tipped tails.

REDBELLY SNAKES

Wriggling across the forest floor, a redbelly snake flicks out its tongue to smell the air. Its tongue forks at the end into two tips. The snake doesn't really smell with its tongue, but the tips bring odors from the air into two tiny pockets at the top of its mouth. These pockets help the snake smell what's nearby.

As you might guess, redbelly snakes are named for their red bellies. But their bellies aren't always red. The bellies can be orange or yellow, and sometimes they're even black. The snakes' backs have brown scales with either thin, dark stripes or one wide, light stripe. The snake's scales aren't slimy. They feel smooth and dry if you touch them. The slippery scales help woodland snakes move smoothly over grass and logs.

Redbelly snakes creep into secret hiding places underneath rocks and logs. They eat worms and slugs, and they stay away from big birds and animals that like to eat snakes. If an enemy comes close, the redbelly snake will roll on its back and pretend to be dead. When the enemy leaves, the sneaky redbelly squiggles away.

GREAT GRAY OWLS

Perched on a low branch in a pine tree, a great gray owl watches the forest floor with two bright, yellow eyes. The owl's eyes seem bigger than they really are because they're surrounded by a circle of flattened feathers.

The owl has hidden ears on the sides of its head, and it can hear high-pitched noises that most humans can't detect. Because it can only see straight ahead, the owl must turn its head to see in different directions. But even in the blackest night, the great gray can see animals moving below. In fact, owls see as well in the dark as humans do in daylight.

Great gray owls are the largest owls in North America. They look especially big because their gray, white, and black feathers are so fluffy. Great grays need these thick feathers to stay warm in winter.

WHO LIVES HERE?

Snug in the long-needled branches of a tall pine, a great gray owl hoots at the nighttime forest. A lynx moves quietly below, leaping over logs and mossy rocks on its large, furry feet. A redbelly snake rustles over broken twigs and curls past fallen pine cones. A lazy porcupine has settled into a wide branch on its favorite tree. The porcupine chews a piece of bark, then settles in for a long nap.

BROADLEAF FORESTS

Broadleaf trees have big, broad leaves. They're called *hardwoods* because the wood from many broadleafs is hard and strong. People use hardwood like oak to build houses and furniture. Because the leaves of nearly all broadleaf trees fall off each autumn, they're also called *deciduous trees*. The word "deciduous" means "to fall off."

In spring, new leaves begin as tiny green buds. The buds uncurl and grow into the specially shaped leaves of each kind of tree. Along with leaves, some broadleaf trees grow flowers, nuts, and fruit.

Most broadleafs change color with the seasons. As the air chills in the fall, orange, scarlet, and yellow-brown leaves flutter to the ground, and the broadleaf forest floor is covered with a crunchy, multi-colored blanket.

RUFFED GROUSE

On a spring morning, a ruffed grouse climbs on top of a fallen log in the forest. The log is covered with patches of green moss and tangles of branches.

The grouse presses his fan-shaped tail against the log and spreads out his wings. He flaps them forward, beating the air faster and faster. *Thump, thump, ump, ump, prrrrr.* When the ruffed grouse drums his wings, the noise sounds like a motor in the distance, or a far-off thunderstorm.

Drumming helps a male grouse find a mate. If a female grouse comes to see what all the noise is about, the male walks toward her with his reddish-gray tail feathers spread outward. He flares the black feathers on his neck, shakes his head, and runs forward with his wings dragging along the forest floor. If the female chooses the male, then the two grouse become mates.

Ruffed grouse eat buds, leaves, fruit, seeds, and insects. They peck at their food like chickens. In the winter, ruffed grouse stay warm by diving into snowbanks. Under a thick blanket of white snow, the grouse is warmer than it is in the open air. If the snow is deep and the wind is cold, most of the grouse's day is spent "snow roosting."

GRAY FOXES

Running past shrubs and trees, a big yellow dog chases a small gray fox. As the fox races ahead, it jumps up a tree trunk and climbs out on a thick branch. Flattening itself against the branch and hiding in the leaves, the fox watches the dog sniff the ground below. When the dog gives up and heads home, the clever gray fox climbs down the tree and escapes.

Like wolves and coyotes, foxes belong to the dog family. But the gray fox is the only dog that can climb trees, so it's sometimes called the tree fox. In fact, a gray fox hunts by hiding on tree branches and pouncing on smaller animals when they walk by. Like other foxes, the gray fox eats rabbits, squirrels, mice, fruits, and berries. But it will also eat bird eggs or baby birds that it finds in tree branches.

Of all the foxes, the gray fox is the best fighter. Males fight with each other. After a few minutes of snarling and biting, one or both of the fighting foxes may walk away with torn ears or cut noses.

WOODPECKERS

As it flies through the forest, the pileated woodpecker's bright red cap of feathers flashes in the sunshine. It lands on a tall aspen and hops up one side of the tree. Tilting its head close to the trunk, the woodpecker listens for insects beneath the bark. It leans back on its stiff black tail and starts to pound the tree with its sharp bill.

Rat-a-tat-tat! Like a feathered hammer, its head bobs up and down. The loud tapping sounds like someone is chopping wood. (Someone is—it's the woodpecker.) The woodpecker's pointed bill makes a tiny hole in the tree. Into the hole goes its long, sticky tongue. Out of the hole come ants, beetles, and white grubs, wiggling on the bird's tongue.

After its meal, the woodpecker rustles its black wings and flies to a birch tree, where its mate is pecking a big, oval-shaped hole into the wood. For almost a month, the two woodpeckers have chiseled away at the tree, making a deep nesting hole that reaches two feet into the tree. Woodpeckers carve new nesting holes into trees every year. Sometimes squirrels, owls, and other birds live in the old woodpecker holes.

WOODLAND JUMPING MICE

Under the silvery light of the moon, the woodland jumping mouse scurries along the forest floor. It creeps under leaves and logs, looking for insects to eat. The woodland mouse's whiskers twitch as it sniffs for enemies. Look out! A sneaky weasel jumps out from under a fern. But with a few long leaps, the woodland jumping mouse escapes. Like a tiny kangaroo with a white-tipped tail, it jumps fast and far.

Because they have long tails and big hind feet that are very strong, woodland jumpers can leap up to eight feet. Most often, they jump in a zig-zag pattern to escape hungry weasels, foxes, hawks, and owls.

Unlike most mice, woodland jumpers hibernate during the winter. They fill themselves with berries, seeds, nuts, and insects in the autumn, until they get very fat. Crawling into their underground burrows, the mice sleep for half the year. When spring comes, they're no longer fat and they're no longer sleepy. They're just hungry. They scoot out of their burrows and crawl up a berry bush, ready to eat lots of fruit and seeds.

WHO LIVES HERE?

The broadleaf forest can be a noisy place. Wind rustles and crackles through the leaves. Woodpeckers hammer on tree trunks, searching for insects to eat. Atop a fallen log, a ruffed grouse drums the air with its wings. The grouse flies up with a *whirr* and hides behind a clump of shrubs. A broad-winged hawk whistles as it swoops downward, and a woodland jumping mouse leaps and scurries under a thatch of ferns. Two gray fox pups scuffle in a bed of fallen leaves, yapping and growling as they play.

MIXED FORESTS

A mixed forest is made up of both needleleaf and broadleaf trees. Sometimes the different trees grow side by side. Other times, one kind of tree grows very tall, while another kind grows below, in the shade of the taller trees.

You can identify most trees by the shape of their leaves, or by the color and feel of their bark. Bark is like a tree's skin, protecting the inside of the tree from harm. Some bark grows as fast as the rest of the tree grows. Other bark grows more slowly than the inside of the tree. That bark becomes cracked and rough, like the bark of pine trees.

FLYING SQUIRRELS

From a high branch in a broadleaf tree, a flying squirrel looks down on the forest floor. Its eyes are big and black. Its fur is soft and silky. Its tail is flat instead of bushy. The squirrel bobs its little head up and down, searching for a spot to land. Then it jumps off the branch.

The flying squirrel sails through the air like a tiny glider. Its four legs are spread out wide, and the loose skin between them stretches out like the top of a parachute. By moving its legs and tail, the squirrel is able to avoid hitting tree trunks and branches.

Just before it lands on the ground, the squirrel raises its tail and lifts its head. Then it lands softly on all four feet. The first thing the squirrel does is scoot up the trunk of a nearby tree. It's hiding from enemies—predators like raccoons, skunks, and owls.

The scientific name of the flying squirrel means "gray mouse that flies." But flying squirrels don't really fly—they glide. Unlike airplanes and birds, flying squirrels can't fly upward. They can only climb up trees and glide gracefully down to the ground.

PINE MARTENS

Leaping from branch to branch high above the forest floor, a pine marten chases a squirrel. The marten follows the squirrel onto a tree limb that ends in a burst of needles, and the clever squirrel seems to disappear. The pine marten twitches her tiny, pointed black nose and her long black whiskers. She looks for the squirrel with her round black eyes, but the smaller animal has already scampered onto another tree.

Finally, the marten gives up and climbs down the tree. On the ground, she catches a small gray mouse. She carries the mouse back to her den. Inside an old tree stump lined with leaves and moss, her two kits whine for food. The mother marten gives her babies the mouse, and helps them find insects to eat near the den.

Pine martens are members of the weasel family. They're fast runners and good climbers. They chase after hares, squirrels, chipmunks, mice, and birds, but they also eat fish, eggs, insects, nuts, and fruit. In the winter, hungry pine martens have to tunnel under the snow to find food. Long hairs grow between their toe pads to keep their feet from getting cold. Their soft, thick fur and long, bushy tails help them stay warm all winter long.

TIMBER WOLVES

Pointing its nose at the dark night sky and opening its mouth, a big gray wolf starts to howl. Soon there's another howl, and another, until seven timber wolves are wagging their tails and howling. Each wolf sings a different note, and the forest fills with their cries. *Ahhwoooo!*

Howling is one of the ways that wolves talk, and the biggest wolf in the pack is usually the first one to make noise. He's the leader. He holds his long, bushy tail up higher than any other wolf. His ears stand up and his fur fluffs out. He's the one who decides whether the pack will hunt or rest.

Most wolves live and hunt together in packs. The pack is like a family. It's made up of the male leader, his mate, their pups, and a few other wolves. Usually only the leader and his mate have pups, but all the wolves in the pack feed and play with the young ones. Older wolves take turns "pup-sitting" while the others go out to find food for the hungry pups.

Wolves are members of the dog family. Like dogs, they have a good sense of smell. With their twitching black noses, they sniff the forest floor when they hunt. Because they work as a team, wolves can hunt animals that are bigger, quicker, and stronger than they are. They often eat deer, caribou, or even moose.

GOSHAWKS

Flying low to the ground, over and under a maze of tangled forest branches, a fierce goshawk chases a red squirrel. Even though the squirrel is fast and clever, the goshawk doesn't give up. His rounded wings help him make quick turns, and his long tail helps him steer around tree trunks and branches. Now, dropping to the ground like a stone, the goshawk screeches. He grabs the squirrel in his sharp talons.

The father goshawk flies back to a big nest made of sticks and built on a high tree branch. Here, he feeds his three fuzzy babies. The nestlings squawk and hop and flap their wings as they fight for food. The mother goshawk helps feed them. She keeps the nestlings warm, too, and protects them from large birds and hungry weasels.

Goshawks are among the fiercest of birds. They're sharp-eyed hunters, and they can fly just by flapping their wings a few times and gliding through the air. Most hawks soar only in wide open spaces, but the goshawk uses its short, powerful wings to fly easily through forests.

WHO LIVES HERE?

The forest has different levels, just like a house or an apartment building. The leafy tops of the tallest trees form the forest's *canopy*. A goshawk makes its nest high in these branches.

Just below the canopy, the treetops and tangled branches of shorter trees make up the *understory*. Pine martens leap from limb to limb, and small flying squirrels parachute to the ground below.

The smallest trees and bushes form the *shrub layer* of the forest. Here, birds and bears look for berries to eat, and timber wolves hide as they stalk and hunt.

The *herb layer* is where grasses, ferns, and wildflowers grow. These plants make good hiding spots for fawns, rabbits, and small animals of the forest.

Beneath everything is the *forest floor*. At this level, trees are rooted in the ground. Here, mice scamper, snakes slither, and insects crawl. Seeds fall and sprout, and new trees start to grow.

WHO LIVES WHERE?

PORCUPINES

Porcupines live in Canada, Alaska, and the
northern and western parts of the United States.

LYNX

Lynx live in the evergreen forests of Canada,
the northern United States, and Alaska.

REDBELLY SNAKES

Redbelly snakes live in the eastern United States.

GREAT GRAY OWLS

Great gray owls are residents of Canada,
Alaska, and the northwestern United States.

RUFFED GROUSE

Ruffed grouse live in southern Canada,
the northern United States, and parts of Alaska.

GRAY FOXES

Gray foxes live throughout most of the United States. The only places
you can't find them are in Alaska, Hawaii, and the northwestern U.S.

PILEATED WOODPECKERS

Pileated woodpeckers live in southern Canada and the eastern
United States. You can also find them in parts of the northwestern U.S.

WOODLAND JUMPING MICE

Woodland jumping mice live in the forests
of southeastern Canada and the northeastern United States.

FLYING SQUIRRELS

Flying squirrels live in Canada, Alaska,
and the northern and eastern United States.

PINE MARTENS

You can find pine martens in Canada,
Alaska, and throughout the northern United States.

TIMBER WOLVES

Most timber wolves live in Canada and Alaska, but you can
also find them in Montana, Michigan, Minnesota, and Wisconsin.

GOSHAWKS

In the springtime, goshawks live in Canada, Alaska, and the northern
United States. They spend the winter in the southern U.S. and Mexico.